INTRODUCTION

This little book is written to inspire imagination, curiosity and the desire to investigate and try to understand life other than being a human being. All my stories show that all creatures share some of the same problems, whether humans or animals.

Dedication

This book is dedicated to all the folks that supported me, especially my wife Donna, and for her illustrations in this book. I also would like to dedicate this book to all readers young and old wherever you are. Thank you.

Designed by Kopi Ko, Lethbridge AB

Long, long ago in Scotland someone saw, or thought they saw, the Loch Ness monster. A short time ago, someone saw, or thought they saw, Ogo Pogo in Okanagan Lake. Only a little while ago we found out about Marapogo, Maralilly, and Maraschino. These three beautiful and seldom seen lake serpents are distant relatives of the Loch Ness monster, and the Ogopogo. They live in the deepest part of Mara Lake which connects to the Shuswap Lake, which connects to one river, then another, and another which probably runs right near by your home.

It seems that we are somewhat scared of things we can't see or seldom see, and we don't understand some creatures and we sometimes call them monsters. In this book there are no monsters, Monster is just a name grown ups give creatures that they know nothing about. More than likely your favorite Lake, has many creatures, all you have to do is listen, believe and let your imagination be free. Try it!

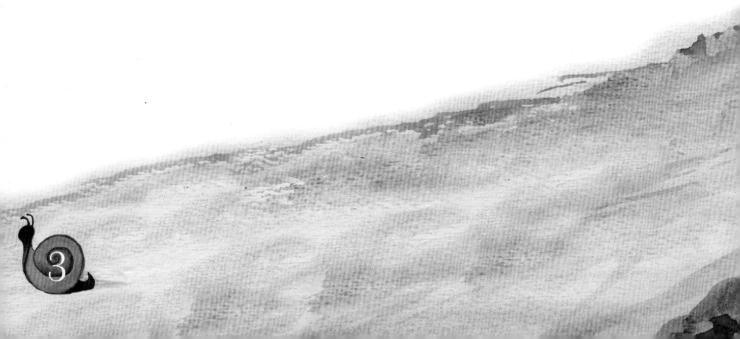

Marapogo, the Dad of the family is kind of a bossy serpent but, fair. He loves the Shuswap and other lakes and rivers and shares the many kilometers of warm and sunny beaches with his family, friends and other creatures.

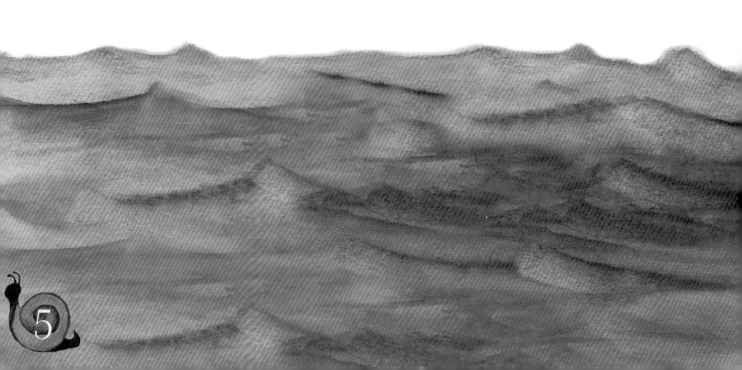

Maralilly, is like all Moms, generous, forgiving, beautiful, warm, with lots of love to give. She also loves the lakes and rivers which is her home and playground. Maralilly feels that all the lakes are here to be shared with all creatures.

8

Maraschino, is a youngster who's not well known. He has a red shiny nose like someone else we know. Maraschino, like all other boys, is adventurous which sometimes gets him into more trouble than he can handle. His most favorite place to play, or just watch and see what's going on is near the light house.

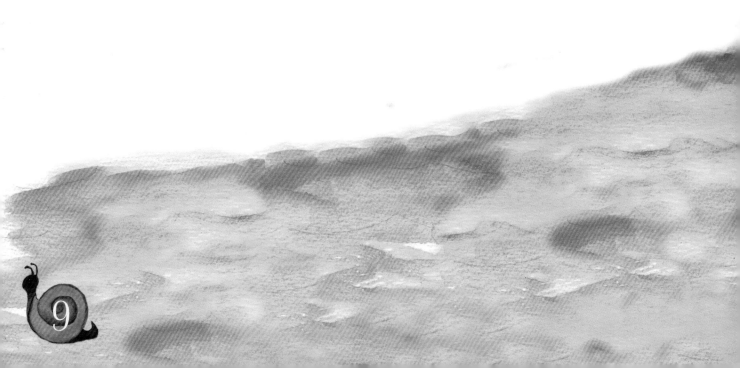

The Serpent family loves to spend time throughout he summer holidays looking for lost soles... soles that are attached to the bottom of boots and shoes, that is.

While thousands of holidayers are having a good time and lying on the beach with their sunglasses on, and their MP3 players plugged into their ears, the serpent family is busy looking for shoes that are not on people's feet. They wouldn't think of taking them off your feet, that would be stealing.

Just like all people that have their special holidays, like first of July, Calgary Stampede, Rose Bowl parade and others, our Serpent friends have a day at the Shuswap Lake called Shoe-Swap day. They love to eat the soles, and keep the rest of the shoes for the lady serpents of the lakes to make hats.

How many of your friends, come home from their holidays with missing shoes, boots, runners and slippers? Now you know the secret of the lost shoes!

Our serpents have a friend, the best of friends you could ever meet but, he is very, very shy. He, like the Loch Ness monster, Ogopogo, or Marapogo, Maralilly and Maraschino, is seldom seen. Because he is so hairy, his favorite time of year is October to March when it is cool, and most of the holidayers have gone back home. Have you guessed his name? It is Broadfoot, some of his relatives are also known as Yeti, or Bigfoot.

Broadfoot is very, very old and wise. There was a time when he was interested in boots and shoes, but when he discovered there were no shoes to fit his feet, he started saving them for his friends the Serpents. He found many shoes on the hiking trails, in roadside ditches, and he found shoes at empty campsites. No one really knows how old Broadfoot and the serpents are, how old is the forest? Maybe that is how old our friends are.

Marapogo, Maralilly, and Maraschino look forward to making plans for Shoe-Swap days. They meet at night along the side of the lake, so if you see a blinking red light it is not a fire truck, or ambulance, nor is it a lighthouse! It's Maraschino's nose! It is Marapogo, Maralilly, Maraschino and their friend Broadfoot discussing and making plans for the big day. Shoe-Swap day on the beautiful Shuswap Lake.

Their favorite place to trade before the big day is were Mara Lake and the Shuswap Lake meet. Have you ever wondered why in some places the water does not freeze, while everything else is frozen? Well that's because our friends Marapogo, Maralilly, Maraschino and Broadfoot are so busy trading shoes and boots for fish, creating currents and waves so strong that the water cannot freeze!

Broadfoot loves the taste of fish and knows fish are very good for him. He truly appreciates the help from his friends, for he is not a very good swimmer, and if he got his fur wet, he would be so heavy that he might drown.

It is a really good and fair trade for the entire Pogo family, Broadfoot and for all of us. By gathering lost shoes everywhere they keep our environment clean and set an example for us to follow. The Pogo family is very happy because they have many types of shoes for their Shoe-Swap day in the Shuswap Lake!

The trading makes Broadfoot very happy, for he gets lots and lots of different kinds of fish which will last him all throughout the winter months.

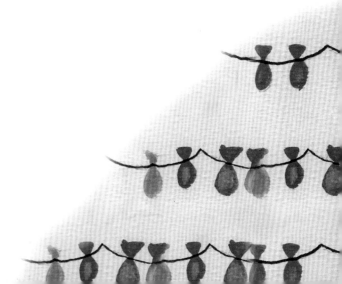

When spring comes, Broadfoot shares the fish with all his animal friends, especially the bears who have been sleeping all winter without eating anything. Broadfoot not only eats the fish, he also uses the bigger skeletons to make his combs and keep himself looking good.

Well it's finally holiday time! You are off to your favorite lake and you're going to have fun.

Whether you're relaxing on the beach, hang gliding, waterskiing, or house boating or going down the Milk River on your rubber raft look out for your friends Marapogo, Maralilly, Maraschino, and don't forget Broadfoot. You just might see them, they love to stop where the houseboats dock for the night, and they love to follow swimmers and boats crossing the lake.

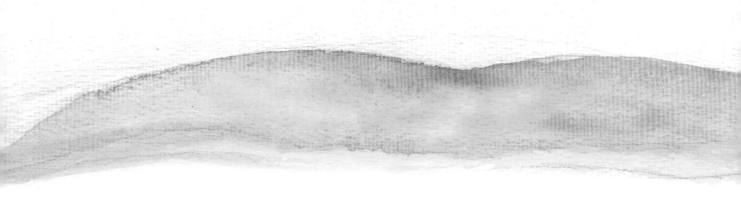

This year when you come on your holiday, remember lakes and rivers are for everyone, man and beast, share them with a friend, and help keep them clean.

If you're walking near a beach or a river with your dog or friends and you spot something that looks like a shoe, chances are that Maraschino and his Mom and Dad and their friend has seen it too.

The End